For Jana and Mimi
—D.T.

For CMdJ
—A.P.

Printed in Malaysia

First Edition, December 2015 • 1 3 5 7 9 10 8 6 4 2 • FAC-029191-15227

Library of Congress Cataloging-in-Publication Data

Teague, David.
  The red hat / by David Teague ; illustrated by Antoinette Portis.—First edition.
    pages cm
  Summary: "Once upon a time, high atop the world, there lived a boy
  named Billy Hightower and the wind. When a new neighbor appears—a girl
  in a red hat—Billy Hightower can hardly wait to meet her and introduce
  himself. But the wind has other ideas"—Provided by publisher.
  ISBN 978-1-4231-3411-4 (hardback)
  [1. Neighbors—Fiction. 2. Winds—Fiction. 3. Perseverance
  (Ethics)—Fiction.] I. Portis, Antoinette, illustrator. II. Title.
  PZ7.T219375Red 2014
  [E]—dc23   2014005679

Reinforced binding

Visit www.DisneyBooks.com

The Red Hat

by David Teague

Illustrated by Antoinette Portis

DISNEY · HYPERION

Los Angeles   New York

Billy Hightower lived atop
the world's tallest building.
Even the clouds didn't reach so high.
When it rained, Billy stayed dry.
No puddles.
No rainbows.

It was the wind

and Billy Hightower.

Until one day a ladder appeared,
followed by men in hard hats, and then . . .

a girl. She wore a red hat.

"Hi. My name

Billy wanted to meet the girl
in the red hat and called out:

is Billy Hightower."

But the wind whisked his words away.

So Billy wrote a note:

Hi. My name is Billy Hightower.
I like your hat.

Then he folded it, and folded it, and folded it,
and threw it to the girl in the red hat.

It glided

and spun.

But before it could reach her,
the wind snatched the note away.

Next Billy tried a kite. On the tail, he wrote:

Hi. My name is Billy Hightower.
I like your hat. The earflaps are nice.

He let it fly.

It climbed.

It dropped.

But
just as the girl
in the red hat
reached for it,
the wind yanked
the kite away.

Billy ran inside
and came back with
a blanket.

Then,
holding the blanket
by the corners,

he captured the wind.

The wind roared.

Billy swooped.

He swirled.

He soared toward the girl

in the red hat.

But just as Billy
reached her . . .

the wind swept him away.

It stole the girl's red hat, too.

When the wind put Billy down

he couldn't see the girl

or the red hat at all.

The wind raged.

It bellowed across boulevards,
trying to drive him back.

"I'm GOING to meet the girl in the red hat," he said.

The wind howled.

It yowled down alleyways, almost stopping him cold.

"... is Billy Hightower."

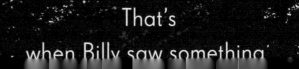

That's
when Billy saw something

After that, the wind didn't stand a chance.

At the elevator, he punched UP,
and he knocked at the first door
on the top floor.

When the girl answered,
Billy took a deep breath and said,
"Hi! My name is Billy Hightower."

Then, with a smile, he added,
"I found your hat."

The Beginning . . .

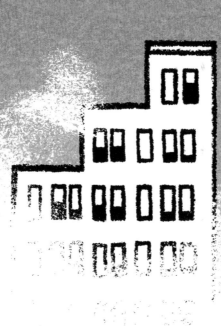